USBORNE FIRST READING
Level Three

For more titles in this series go to
www.usborne.com

Dinosaurs

Conrad Mason

Illustrated by

Daniel Howarth

Reading consultant: Alison Kelly
Roehampton University

Millions of years ago,
incredible creatures
lived on Earth.

Brachiosaurus

They were
dinosaurs.

Stegosaurus

The word dinosaur
means terrible lizard.

Allosaurus

4

Some dinosaurs walked
on two legs.

Gallimimus

Some walked on four legs.

Ankylosaurus

There were lots of different dinosaurs.

Some had spiny backs.

Spinosaurus

Some had bony plates.

←— Plates

Stegosaurus

Some had strange crests.

Corythosaurus

Crest→

←Crest

Tsintaosaurus

Saurolophus

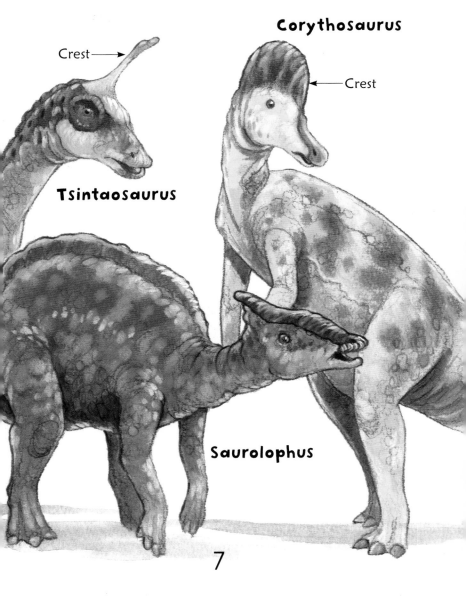

7

These dinosaurs had very big crests.

Parasaurolophus

They probably blew
through them to make
a noise.

Honk!

This dinosaur is called Apatosaurus. It was longer than a bus,

Ornitholestes

taller than
a house,

BOOM!
BOOM!

and as heavy as
four elephants.

Another Ornitholestes

Not all dinosaurs
were so big.

This is Scutellosaurus next
to a modern-day cat.

This tiny dinosaur
was even smaller.
It is called...

Micropachycephalosaurus!

Dinosaurs lived
on the land.

Mussaurus

Two Eoraptors

It was very hot.

Another Mussaurus

Plants grew everywhere.

Pterosaurs looped
and swooped in the sky.

Plesiosaurs splashed
and swam in the sea.

18

Plesiosaur

19

Most dinosaurs
were plant-eaters,
or herbivores.

Stegosaurus

Diplodocus had
a long neck.

It ate leaves high up
in trees.

Some dinosaurs were meat-eaters, or carnivores.

Saurornithoides

Velociraptors

They ate anything they
could catch...

Tarbosaurus

Saurolophus

...even other dinosaurs.
23

Tyrannosaurus rex was
one of the biggest
carnivores.

Dromiceiomimus

It had huge teeth to
crunch and munch bones.

But its arms were tiny.
No one knows why.

25

Some meat-eaters
were small and fast.

Velociraptors

Velociraptors had sharp
claws to grip their victims.

Khaan

Sometimes a meat-eater's
victim escaped.

Tarbosaurus

Gallimimus could
run away fast.

Gallimimus

28

Triceratops had horns to
scare off attackers.

And Iguanodon had
spikes instead of thumbs.

This Ankylosaurus was
very safe indeed. It had
thick plates and a
club on its tail.

If another dinosaur attacked...

Tyrannosaurus rex

THUMP!

31

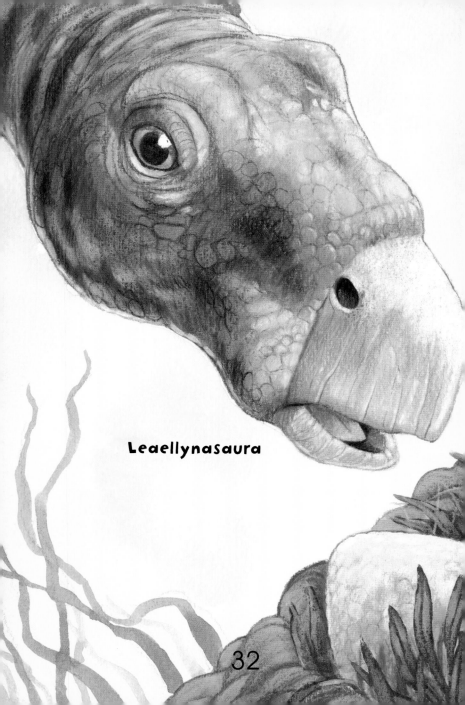

Leaellynasaura

Mother dinosaurs
made nests.

Then they laid eggs.

Baby dinosaurs broke out
of the eggs.

CRACK!

Some went off to
find food.

Orodromeus

Some stayed in the
nest until they
were bigger.

Maiasaura

Dinosaurs lived on earth for more than a hundred million years.

Then almost all of
them disappeared.

Some people think that a big rock fell from space and hit the earth.

Quetzalcoatlus

Edmontosaurus

Triceratops

Dust filled the sky.
It hid the sun.

It was too cold for
dinosaurs to live.

There is a lot we don't
know about dinosaurs.

We don't even know what
their skin looked like.

Perhaps they
were green...

or spotted...

or striped.

Experts find out about
dinosaurs by looking
at fossils.

Fossils are bones
that have turned to stone.

Maybe you will
find a fossil one day.

Dinosaur timeline

Dinosaurs didn't all live at the same time. This timeline shows when different dinosaurs lived.

Triassic period
(245 million years ago)

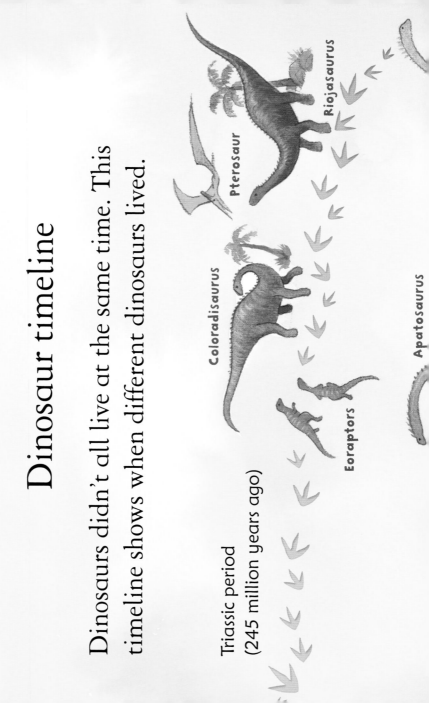

Riojasaurus

Pterosaur

Coloradisaurus

Eoraptors

Apatosaurus

Diplodocus

Jurassic period
(208 million years ago)

Stegosaurus

Allosaurus

Triceratops

Tyrannosaurus rex

Ankylosaurus

Parasaurolophus

Velociraptor

Cretaceous period
(146 million years ago)

Dinosaur glossary

Here are some words in the book that you might not know.

 carnivore – a meat-eating animal

 crest – a part that sticks up on a dinosaur's head

 fossil – bones that have turned to stone

 herbivore – a plant-eating animal

Index

Dinosaur websites

For links to websites where you can find out more about dinosaurs and hear how to say their names, go to the Usborne Quicklinks Website at **www.usborne-quicklinks.com** and type in the keywords "first reading dinosaurs". Please ask an adult before using the internet.

USBORNE FIRST READING
Level Four

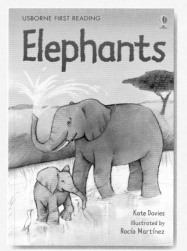

USBORNE FIRST READING

Elephants

Kate Davies
Illustrated by
Rocío Martínez

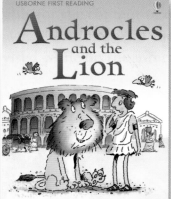

USBORNE FIRST READING

Androcles
and the
Lion

Retold by Russell Punter
Illustrated by Mike and Carl Gordon

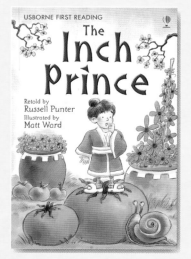

USBORNE FIRST READING

The
Inch
Prince

Retold by
Russell Punter
Illustrated by
Matt Ward

USBORNE FIRST READING

Owls

Sarah Courtauld
Illustrated by Lorna Hussey